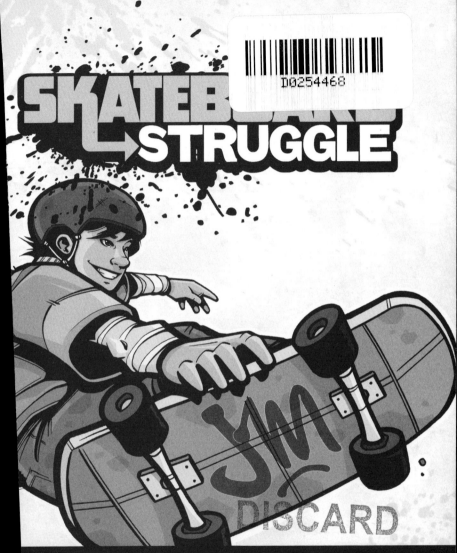

SKATEBOARD STRUGGLE

BY JAKE MADDOX

TEXT BY
THOMAS KINGSLEY TROUPE

ILLUSTRATIONS BY
SEAN TIFFANY

STONE ARCH BOOKS
a capstone imprint

Jake Maddox books are published by Stone Arch Books
A Capstone Imprint
151 Good Counsel Drive, P.O. Box 669
Mankato, Minnesota 56002
www.capstonepub.com

Library of Congress Cataloging-in-Publication Data
Maddox, Jake.
  Skateboard struggle / by Jake Maddox ; text by Thomas Kingsley Troupe ;
illustrated by Sean Tiffany.
      p. cm. -- (Jake Maddox sports story)
  Summary: Despite his parents' ban on skateboarding, Evan is determined to
prepare for a competition-- should he continue in secret or tell his parents the
truth?
  ISBN 978-1-4342-2987-8 (library binding) -- ISBN 978-1-4342-3424-7 (pbk.)
  1. Skateboarding--Juvenile fiction. 2. Family life--Juvenile fiction. [1.
Skateboarding--Fiction. 2. Family life--Fiction.] I. Troupe, Thomas Kingsley. II.
Tiffany, Sean, ill. III. Title.
  PZ7.M25643Ske 2011
  [Fic]--dc22
                                    2011000348

Art Director: Kay Fraser
Graphic Designer: Russell Griesmer
Production Specialist: Michelle Biedscheid

Photo Credits: Sean Tiffany (cover)

Printed in the United States of America in Stevens Point, Wisconsin.
112011
006455R

TABLE OF CONTENTS

CHAPTER 1
BEING CAREFUL...............5

CHAPTER 2
HALF TRUTHS...............11

CHAPTER 3
BROTHER BOTHER...............17

CHAPTER 4
A TEMPTING OFFER...............21

CHAPTER 5
THE EGGPLANT...............27

CHAPTER 6
CAUGHT!...............34

CHAPTER 7
GRANDMA'S GIFT...............40

CHAPTER 8
THE SKATE-OFF...............46

CHAPTER 9
SURPRISE SPECTATORS...............52

CHAPTER 10
TAKING THE RISK...............57

CHAPTER 1

BEING CAREFUL

Evan Narita looked nervously over his shoulder as he walked into the skate park. All around the park, the usual groups of skateboarders were on the halfpipes and grinding on the rails.

He waved at his friend Ryan Thompson, who was waiting for him near the edge of the park.

"You made it," Ryan said. "Are you sure nobody followed you here?"

"Very funny," Evan replied. "If my parents catch me, I'm toast. But no, smart guy, no one followed me."

Even so, Evan couldn't help glancing at the sidewalks around the park. He didn't see anyone from his family, but he could never be too careful.

Two months ago, Evan's older brother, Chris, had broken his leg while skateboarding. Chris had been trying a risky lip trick on a halfpipe when he fell. He hadn't been wearing pads.

Evan's parents had decided that skateboarding was too dangerous. And ever since then, no one in the Narita family was allowed to do it. The problem was that all of Evan's friends were boarders. They all hung out at the skate park.

Evan loved skateboarding. He couldn't just quit. He kept skating. But the park was only four blocks from his house, and he was worried he'd get caught.

Ryan kicked his board up, caught it, and handed it to Evan. "Here you go," Ryan said. "You might as well get in some deck time before they catch you."

"Very funny," Evan muttered. He felt dumb. He didn't even have his own skateboard anymore. After Chris's accident, their parents had gotten rid of both boys' boards. Now Evan had to borrow Ryan's board.

"Did you bring the gear?" Evan asked, pointing to the backpack near Ryan's feet.

"Yep," Ryan said. He tossed it over. "Here it is."

Inside Ryan's backpack were elbow pads, kneepads, and a helmet. Everything was covered in skateboard logo stickers. After Chris's accident, Evan wasn't taking any chances.

The other skaters who didn't wear as much gear probably thought Evan was too careful, but he didn't care. Broken bones kept skaters off skateboards. Sometimes for good.

Evan opened the bag and started pulling on the pads. Within minutes, he was geared up.

"Thanks for bringing all this stuff," Evan said. He stepped onto the skateboard. "If I went home hurt, my parents would definitely know something is up. They'd probably ground me forever."

Evan pushed away from Ryan. The board rolled along the ground and made the *click-clack* sound he liked. He did a manual, followed by a kickflip. He landed smoothly back on the deck both times.

Evan made his way to the top of a ramp, pausing for a second before dropping in. He balanced the back edge of the board on the edge with the wheels dangling over. The nose of the board faced up. Evan kept one foot on the back of the board to hold it in place. Then he placed his other foot at the front of the board and dropped in to the ramp.

Evan was pretty good at skateboarding, but he knew he still had room for improvement. *If I could practice on the driveway and on my way to school, I'd be way better*, he thought.

Evan glanced at the sidewalk once more before rolling into the skate park. Ryan jogged behind him.

"Ten minutes and then we switch," Ryan said. "I'm timing you, pal."

"Got it," Evan said. He gave Ryan a thumbs-up.

I've got to make every minute count, Evan thought. *I really need my own board.*

CHAPTER 2

HALF TRUTHS

When it started to get dark, Evan was forced to cut his last turn short. He reluctantly hopped off of Ryan's skateboard and handed it back.

"I need to get home for dinner," Evan said to Ryan. "My parents are going to wonder where I am." He glanced down at his watch. 6:15! It was much later than he'd thought. He pulled off the helmet and pads and tossed them to Ryan.

"You've got helmet hair, dude," Ryan said. He pointed to Evan's dark hair. "Mess it up or something."

Evan ran a hand through his hair. It felt sweaty. Running home would make him even sweatier. He glanced around the skate park again, but he knew no one from his family would be outside. Everyone was home, sitting at the table, waiting for him.

"I've got to fly, Ryan," Evan said. "See you tomorrow."

"Sure thing," Ryan said. He waved Evan away. "Now get home before you're grounded!"

* * *

Evan burst through the back door, scaring his grandmother. She jumped and muttered something in Japanese.

"Sorry, *obaasan*," Evan said. He didn't speak much Japanese, but he'd picked up a couple of words. Ever since his grandmother had moved in, Japanese was spoken more often around the house.

Grandma Narita, unfortunately, didn't speak any English.

"Evan?" his father called from the dining room. "Come and sit with us at once. We've been waiting for you long enough!"

Evan hurried to the dinner table. His parents, along with Chris, were seated with plates of food in front of them.

"Sorry I'm late," Evan said. He quickly sat down.

"Where were you?" his mother asked. She passed him a bowl of salad.

"I was at the park with Ryan," Evan said. He hoped his parents wouldn't ask which park. "I lost track of time."

Evan glanced at Chris, who shook his head. Only Chris knew his secret. But Evan knew that his brother wouldn't say anything.

"You need to pay more attention to the time," his father said. "We eat at six o'clock every night, no exceptions."

"Maybe next time we should have a picnic dinner at the park," Chris joked. "Then Evan would be on time."

Evan's family laughed. Even his grandmother, who didn't know what Chris had said.

"You're all sweaty," Evan's mother said. "Were you running a marathon?"

As Evan ate his dinner, he felt his parents watching him. *Do they know I'm secretly skateboarding?* he thought.

Evan took a gulp of water, then shook his head. "Oh, no," he said, trying to sound casual. "I just ran home."

"Too bad you didn't have something to ride back here," Chris said. He pointed a breadstick at his younger brother. "It's easier to get home when you've got a set of wheels."

Very funny, Evan thought.

"I'll remember that next time," he said, giving his brother a dirty look.

CHAPTER 3

BROTHER BOTHER

After helping his parents clear the table, Evan excused himself. He headed to his room to finish his homework. Chris followed him up the stairs. It was hard for him to keep up with Evan since his leg was still in a cast.

"What would Mom and Dad do if they saw you at the skate park?" Chris asked. He flopped onto Evan's bed and looked up at the ceiling.

"We'll never know, because they'll never know," Evan said. He sat down at his desk and opened his textbook to start reading.

"But still," Chris said. "After my accident, they said no one in this house could skate."

"Stop talking about it," Evan interrupted. He turned around at his desk. "If they hear you talking about it, they'll figure it out."

"You mean skateboarding?" Chris said loudly. Evan jumped up and closed his bedroom door.

"It's not my fault you broke your leg," Evan whispered. "You're the reason no one else in this family can skate."

Chris smiled. "I'm just joking around," he said. "Relax."

"You haven't told them, have you?" Evan asked. He glanced at the door, sure his mom or dad would open it any second.

"No way," Chris said, shaking his head. "If you get caught, it'll be your own fault."

That doesn't make me feel any better, Evan thought.

"I won't get caught," Evan said. "Besides, I'm always careful."

"So was I," Chris said. He used his crutches to struggle to his feet and turned to leave. But before he opened the door, he turned to Evan and added, "Then I ended up with a broken leg."

CHAPTER 4

A TEMPTING OFFER

An hour later, Evan finished his biology reading. He answered his chapter questions and packed his books for school. Then he carefully slid a magazine out of his desk drawer.

It was *Skate Stunts*, a skateboard tricks magazine Ryan got in the mail. Whenever Ryan finished reading an issue, he let Evan borrow it. It was the only chance Evan had to read up on new tricks.

It made him nervous to keep anything skateboard-related in the house, so he hid the magazines well. He made sure his door was closed, then flopped down on his bed and looked through the magazine.

There were some amazing tricks in this issue. The skateboard pros always made the tricks look easy. Evan read about a trick called "The Eggplant." It was a hand-plant trick. As a boarder approached the lip of a ramp, he had to plant his hand on the spine. His back hand stayed on the board, between his legs. Then he extended as far as possible before landing and riding away.

Evan pictured himself trying the trick in front of his friends. Then his bedroom door burst open.

"What are you reading, Evan?" a stern voice boomed from the doorway.

His heart pounding, Evan sat up. He stuffed the magazine underneath his pillow.

"You should see the look on your face," Chris said. He pointed at Evan and laughed. "I think you jumped about five feet in the air."

"You're not even a little bit funny," Evan said. It took him a moment to settle down. He'd been so sure he was busted. Chris came into his room. He was holding a bright orange piece of paper.

"Did you see this?" Chris asked. He showed the paper to Evan.

Evan was still mad, but the flier caught his eye. It showed a cartoon skateboarder high in the air. The paper read, "1st Annual Skate-Off: Shaffer Skate Park."

"Let me see that," Evan said. He stood up and snatched the paper from Chris's hand. The flier said there was no entry fee and all ages were welcome. The competition was on a Saturday next month.

"Where did you get this?" Evan demanded. "Mom and Dad will freak if they find this in the house."

"Relax," Chris said. "I found it in the mail and grabbed it before anyone saw it. Are you thinking of signing up?"

"No way," Evan said, tossing the flier aside. "It's too risky. Besides, I don't even have a skateboard anymore." But the truth was, it did sound like fun. He wondered if Ryan and the other guys knew about the competition.

Chris shrugged. "I guess you're right," he said. "I just thought you'd want to know about it." Then, he turned and limped back out of the room.

After Chris left, Evan picked up the flier. He looked at it once more before crumpling the paper. He tossed it perfectly into the garbage can.

Maybe I should take up basketball, Evan thought.

CHAPTER 5

THE EGGPLANT

After school the next day, Evan found Ryan sitting on the front steps of their school, waiting for him.

"Hey," Ryan said as Evan walked up. "Did you see this?" He pulled out an orange piece of paper. It was a flier for the Skate-Off.

"Yes," Evan said, groaning. "Don't remind me. Chris showed it to me last night at home."

"You should enter," Ryan said. "You're one of the best skaters around."

"Yeah right," Evan said. "I'm okay, but I'm nowhere near as good as some of the other guys. Besides, I don't have a board."

"You could use my board," Ryan offered. "If the judges let us share."

Evan thought about it for a minute. Then he shook his head. "I can't," he said. "It's bad enough that I skate in secret. Entering a contest is just asking to get caught."

Ryan pointed to the flier. "It's at Shaffer Park," he said. "That's all the way on the other side of town. How would your parents ever find out?"

Evan was quiet. "I don't know," he said finally. "I'll think about it."

The two boys walked to the bike rack. They hopped on their bikes and headed to the skate park. As they biked, Evan thought about the Skate-Off. Competing was sounding better and better.

Maybe I should enter, Evan thought. *It's just one competition. What's the worst that could happen?*

* * *

After half an hour at the skate park, Evan realized he wasn't the only one thinking about competing. It seemed like every boarder there was planning to enter. Even though it made him nervous, Evan decided to enter, too.

"I hope they let us share skateboards," Evan said. "If I need my own, I'm out."

"I'm sure they'll let us share," Ryan said.

"I might have an old one you can borrow," another skateboarder offered. Everyone knew about the ban Evan's parents had put on skateboarding.

"Thanks," Evan said. "Now let's get to work. If I'm entering this thing, I need the practice."

Evan and Ryan went back and forth, trading the skateboard and working on the basics. They tried to grind the rails over and over again. Halfway through one grind, Evan lost his balance and had to bail.

"Easy on the deck," Ryan shouted from the top of the halfpipe. "Neither of us will be able to compete if you break it!"

When his turn was over, Evan watched the other guys. All the boarders were trying their most difficult moves.

Then Evan remembered the trick he'd seen in the magazine. The eggplant. It had looked tricky, but Evan wondered if he could do it.

There was only one way to find out.

It'll be easy, Evan thought. But he was a little nervous. The pros always made tricks look easy. But they rarely were.

Evan rolled up the halfpipe and reverted to roll back down. Gaining speed, he aimed for the spine of the ramp. He crouched low and put out his front hand.

When he was close, he reached for the spine. Evan's hand touched the metal along the top, and he slipped.

The board rolled one way, and Evan went down, face first, onto the ramp. A total wipeout!

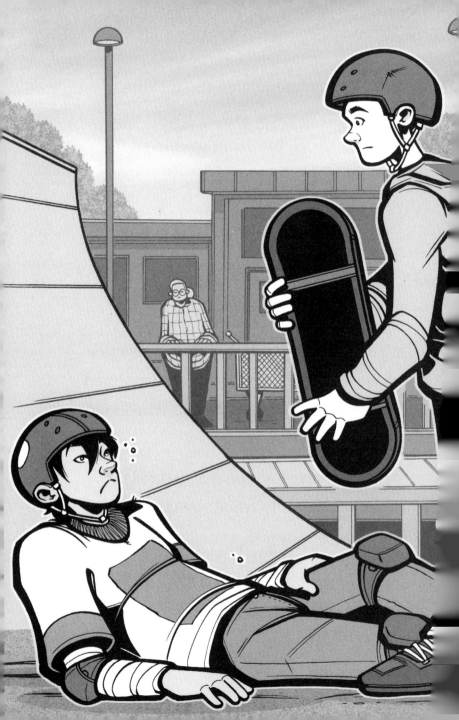

"Nice!" one of the guys shouted.

Evan rolled onto his back and stared up at the sky. "Looks like it's not going to be as easy as I thought," he muttered. The eggplant would take practice. He sat up and saw Ryan snatch up his escaping skateboard.

"What were you trying to do?" Ryan asked. He checked his board for damage. "That looked like a face plant."

"Close," Evan said. He got to his feet. "It was supposed to be an eggplant, but . . ."

Evan didn't finish his sentence. Something near the skate-park entrance caught his eye.

An older woman stood there, watching him. Evan squinted. Then he realized he knew her. It was his grandmother!

CHAPTER 6

CAUGHT!

"Oh, man. I'm in trouble," Evan mumbled. He stripped off his elbow pads and looked again.

There was no mistake. It was his grandmother, standing in her red plaid coat and pushing her small grocery cart. She waved at her grandson. Evan slowly waved back.

"Oh, wow," Ryan said. "That's your grandma, isn't it? This isn't good."

"No kidding," Evan said. "And the worst part? I don't even know how to tell her not to tell my parents. She doesn't speak English."

Evan quickly removed the rest of the pads. Then he jogged over to his grandmother.

"Good luck!" Ryan called from behind. Evan barely heard him. He was too busy thinking about was how much trouble he was in.

"Hello, Grandma," Evan said. Then remembered how to say it in Japanese. "*Kon'nichiwa, obaasan.*"

Grandma Narita smiled. She murmured something in Japanese that Evan couldn't understand. He nodded and walked along the sidewalk with her.

"I'm not sure how to explain this, Grandma," Evan said. He took the cart's handle to help push her groceries home. "But please don't tell my parents I was skateboarding."

Grandma Narita replied again in Japanese. She didn't seem confused by what he said. She put a finger up, nodded, and smiled again.

This isn't working, Evan thought. *She probably thinks I'm asking about dinner or something. She has no idea what I'm saying.*

Evan stopped walking and let go of the cart. Grandma stopped too, frowning.

With his hand held out flat, Evan used his other hand to show a person. He made the finger-person walk by wiggling his pointer and middle fingers.

Grandma nodded and gave Evan an unsure smile.

Evan tried to show the finger-person skateboarding on his hand. He cupped his other hand to make it look like a halfpipe.

"Please," Evan said. He shook his head and pointed to his mouth. "Don't talk about skateboarding."

Grandma replied in Japanese and nodded. Evan still wasn't sure that she understood what he was saying.

"My parents," Evan said and pointed down the street toward their house. "They can't know I skateboard."

Trying to make her understand, Evan made his hands into a skateboard and halfpipe again. He shook his head to show it was forbidden.

Grandma looked down toward the Narita house and then back at Evan. She put her small hands over her grandson's. She nodded and patted Evan on the cheek. Then she smiled and said something in Japanese.

I think she understands, Evan thought and smiled back. He took the grocery cart and headed toward the house with his grandmother. He hoped she'd keep her promise.

The truth was, Evan wasn't exactly sure she'd even made a promise. Maybe Grandma would just forget what she'd seen. Evan's freedom and skateboarding career depended on it.

CHAPTER 7

GRANDMA'S GIFT

A week went by, and Evan still wasn't grounded. No one, not even Chris, mentioned skateboarding. It seemed like Grandma Narita had kept up her end of the bargain. Evan was starting to wonder if maybe Grandma could understand English after all.

But when Evan entered his bedroom Friday evening, he realized she hadn't understood him. Not one bit.

"You have to be kidding me," Evan said, his mouth dropping open. He stood in the doorway of his bedroom and dropped his backpack onto the floor. He blinked twice to make sure he wasn't dreaming.

There on his bed, for the entire world to see, was a brand-new skateboard. A small white card lay on top of the deck.

"Oh, Grandma," Evan whispered. "What have you done?"

Evan heard someone coming upstairs, so he moved quickly. He grabbed his bag, closed the door, and dashed to his bed. He eyed the skateboard and sighed. It had new grip tape on the deck and a cool dragon graphic on the underside. The rest of the board was covered in cool-looking blue and red flames.

Evan grabbed the card and opened it. Inside were Japanese characters, written in his grandma's small handwriting. Though he didn't understand them, Evan realized what his grandma meant.

Grandma thought I was asking for a skateboard, Evan thought. Somehow his hand movements had delivered a completely different message than he'd intended.

Then, outside his door, he heard footsteps.

Evan grabbed his new skateboard and slid it under his bed. A second later, the door opened. His father poked his head inside.

"We're making popcorn for a movie," Dad said. "I thought you'd like to join us."

Evan stood up. His heart thumped fast in his chest.

"Sounds good, Dad," Evan said. "I was just finishing up some homework. I'll head down in a second."

His dad smiled. "It's only Friday night, and you're already tackling your school work," Dad said. "You make me proud, Evan."

"Thanks," Evan said. "You know me. I like to get it done right away. It's better than worrying about it all weekend."

"Good thinking," Dad replied. He turned to leave and said, "Don't work too hard. Be sure to leave time for fun and relaxation."

"Oh, I will," Evan said.

Once his dad left, Evan breathed a sigh of relief.

That was close, he thought. After he heard his dad's footsteps on the stairs, he crouched down and pulled the skateboard from under his bed.

It was beautiful, but Evan knew it could get him into deep trouble.

I'll just use it for the Skate-Off, Evan thought. *I'll keep it hidden until I can sneak it out of here. Then it can live at Ryan's house.*

Evan took one last look at the skateboard before sliding it back under his bed. Then he headed downstairs.

His whole family sat in the living room, watching the movie. Evan joined them, but it was hard for him to concentrate. More than anything, he wanted to head to the skate park to try out his new board. It didn't seem fair that it had to stay hidden.

CHAPTER 8

THE SKATE-OFF

Before Evan knew it, Saturday had arrived. The Skate-Off was that afternoon. Luckily, he'd had a chance to practice with his new skateboard a few times after sneaking it out of his room. He'd even landed the eggplant a few times. It wasn't perfect, but it wasn't bad, either.

After lunch, Evan and Ryan rode their bikes all the way to Shaffer Skate Park. Their backpacks were full of skating gear.

The park was busy. "Are you nervous, Evan?" Ryan asked. He kickflipped his board while he waited for his turn.

"A little bit," Evan admitted. In truth, he was more worried about getting caught. "I don't know how this works."

"It's simple," Ryan said. "You get three two-minute runs. Do all your best tricks, and the judges will pick your best session. The highest score wins."

"Wow," Evan said, laughing. "You make it sound so easy."

"I'm up," Ryan said. He headed to the top of the halfpipe to start his first run.

Evan watched Ryan on the halfpipe. He did a lip grind, then reverted, putting one foot on the nose of the board while keeping the other in the middle for balance.

Ryan lifted the tail of the board up slightly before turning it to face the other side. Then he skated back down the slope.

As Ryan headed toward the pyramid, Evan looked into the crowd. A lot of people gathered around the skate park to watch. Most of the spectators were younger kids, but Evan spotted a few adults.

An air horn signaled the end of Ryan's first run. He hopped off the deck and flipped it up into his hand.

"I didn't do so well," Ryan said when he walked back to where Evan stood. "I'm not used to the ramps here."

"I probably won't do much better," Evan said. He and Ryan stood on the sidelines watching a few more skaters take their turns. Then it was Evan's turn.

"Are you ready?" Ryan asked. He clapped Evan on the back. "Your first competition on your new board. This is going to be awesome!"

"Right," Evan said. He laughed. "Probably awesomely bad."

The air horn sounded, and Evan was off. He crouched low to build up speed off of the halfpipe.

He did a varial kickflip, making the board spin around and flip over at the same time. Evan landed on the deck perfectly, just as he reached the other side of the halfpipe.

Not bad so far, Evan thought. He reverted to turn back the other way and did a manual toward the funboxes with rails bolted to them.

Evan ollied up onto the rail. Keeping his feet connected to the board, he did a nose-grind halfway down the pipe. When his balance was shaky, he jumped off and rolled down the ramp.

After a handful of some of his easier tricks, Evan heard the air horn. His session was over.

As he kicked his board up and waved to the clapping crowd, Evan looked around. He saw a group of spectators that made him lose his breath. Standing at the edge of the skate park were five people he recognized.

Oh no, Evan thought.

In the crowd, he saw Chris, Grandma Narita, and . . .

"Mom and Dad," Evan whispered.

CHAPTER 9

SURPRISE SPECTATORS

I'm in so much trouble, Evan thought. He wiped his sweaty palms against his pants. *How did they know I was here?*

Evan walked back to Ryan. He tried not to look, but he could feel his family watching him.

"Nice run," Ryan said. "Not bad for your first competition."

"Too bad it will be my last," Evan said. "I'm busted. My whole family is out there."

Ryan turned and looked.

"Don't look, Ryan!" Evan shouted. "I'm already in enough trouble."

"Why are they here?" Ryan asked.

"I don't know! I didn't say a thing about it to anyone," Evan said, shaking his head. "I even told Chris I wouldn't compete."

"Grandma," both of them said together.

But that didn't make sense either. Grandma Narita thought Evan had asked for a skateboard. *I never said anything about a competition*, Evan thought. *There's no way she could know I'd be here.*

Both Ryan and Evan were quiet for a moment. The next skater started his run.

"What are you going to do?" Ryan asked.

"I should probably quit and accept my punishment," Evan said. He adjusted his elbow pads and clenched his fists. "I can't believe this! I was so careful."

"Or," Ryan said, looking over at the Narita family, "you could finish your runs, and then go over. I mean, you're already in trouble anyway, right?"

Evan glanced over at his family. They were all watching the other skaters. No one seemed to be in a hurry to find him.

"Maybe you're right," Evan said. He wasn't in a hurry to get yelled at. What could it hurt to finish?

* * *

After what seemed like forever, it was Evan's turn again. His second run was a disaster.

He couldn't focus on his tricks, and he bailed three times during his two minutes. When the air horn signaled the end of his run, Evan was relieved.

"It's over," Evan said when he reached Ryan again. "I can't do anything with my parents watching me. They're going to ground me for the rest of my life."

"In case you haven't noticed, Evan, no one is doing that well," Ryan said. "Your first run is still in the top five so far. You could win if you bust out a bigger trick."

Evan groaned. He didn't want to try a third run. The last one had been a mess.

But I could win, Evan thought. *Maybe I should give the eggplant a try.*

"Okay," Evan said. "I'll try something bigger. What have I got to lose?"

CHAPTER 10

TAKING THE RISK

Before Evan knew it, it was time for his final run. The air horn sounded, and Evan hopped onto his board. He raced down the halfpipe and did a heelflip, making the board spin 360 degrees. He landed hard on the deck.

Halfway up the slope, Evan began to slow down. He reverted to face the other direction. Evan crouched down to build up speed and rolled to the spine ramp.

For show, he did a manual, raising his front wheels off the ground. When his balance wavered, he kicked off and headed for the ramp.

I haven't landed a clean eggplant yet, Evan thought. *Why do I think I can do one now?*

Evan tried to forget all of the trouble he was in with his parents. In the minute he had left, he knew he had to try his best.

After all, this is the last time I'll ever get to skateboard, Evan thought. *I might as well make it count.* With a burst of speed, he hit the ramp. Evan reached out and lifted the board between his legs.

Evan smiled. He was going to nail the trick! But suddenly, he lost his hold on the slippery pipe. He fell onto the other side of the ramp and landed hard on his elbow.

His skateboard clattered to the ground nearby as Evan rolled onto his back. He didn't bother to get up and finish the run.

"Evan!" a familiar voice shouted. Evan sat up and looked at the crowd. His family was running toward him. They all looked worried. With a deep breath, Evan stood up. He met them at the edge of the park.

"Are you okay?" Dad asked. He put a hand on Evan's shoulder.

"I'm fine, Dad," Evan said. "The pads did their job."

"I was so worried about you," his mother said. She touched Evan's cheek. "You know how I feel about these skateboards."

Evan nodded and looked at the ground. "I know," he said. "And I'm sorry I didn't tell you. I was afraid you'd be upset."

Dad looked around. "I'd be more upset if you dressed like some of these other skaters," he said. "Some of them aren't even wearing helmets! I'm not happy that you hid this from us, but at least you're being safe."

Evan looked up. "So you're not super mad?" he asked.

"You're doing something you love," Dad said, shaking his head. "I can see that now. And you're good at it. How can I be mad about that? That doesn't mean you're not grounded, though. When we get home, we'll talk about you lying to us."

Evan looked up. The judges had posted his final score. He'd dropped to 12th place. That wasn't good enough to make it into the finals. "Looks like I'm not that good after all," he muttered.

Chris put his arm around his brother. "You did pretty well," Chris said. "After all, this was your first competition. Or was it?"

"It was," Evan said with a smile.

Just then, he remembered something. "I've got to ask," Evan said. "How did you all know I was here?"

Grandma Narita said something in Japanese. Evan's dad replied in her language, and they both laughed. Then Grandma pulled a crumpled piece of orange paper from her purse.

It was the flier for the Skate-Off. The same one Evan had thrown away.

"Grandma told us about the new skateboard she bought you," Mom said. "Then, when I emptied the trash in your room, this caught my eye."

"I'm sorry. I should've said something," Evan said. "I guess I should retire the board now."

Dad shook his head. "You'd better not," he said. "Your grandmother spent a lot of money on that skateboard. It'd be a shame to let it — and your talent — go to waste."

Evan nodded. He couldn't believe how understanding his parents were being. *I should have talked to them about skateboarding a lot sooner*, he realized.

"Thanks, Dad," he said. "Thanks for understanding."

"Does this mean I can skateboard again, too?" Chris interrupted, sounding excited. "I get my cast off soon."

"Oh, boy," Dad said. "Let's talk about it over lunch, okay?"

Evan turned and looked across the park at Ryan. His friend mouthed, *What's up?*

Since he was too far away to say anything, Evan gave Ryan a thumbs-up. Then he pointed to his family to signal he was leaving with them. Ryan smiled and waved.

Turning back around, Evan caught his grandmother's eye. She smiled secretively and gave him the same thumbs-up signal he'd given Ryan.

"Thanks, Grandma," he whispered, smiling at her. "*Arigato.*"

Then Evan picked up his skateboard and left the skate park with his family.

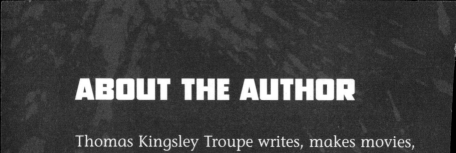

ABOUT THE AUTHOR

Thomas Kingsley Troupe writes, makes movies,

GLOSSARY

accident (AK-sih-duhnt)—an unfortunate and unplanned event

bargain (BAR-guhn)—an agreement between two people

career (kuh-RIHR)—the work or the series of jobs that a person has

competition (com-puh-TISH-uhn)—a contest of some kind

exception (ek-SEP-shuhn)—something that is not included in a general rule or statement

forbidden (for-BID-in)—not allowed

frail (FRAYL)—weak

improvement (im-PROOV-muhnt)—to get better, or to make something better

relaxation (ree-lak-SAY-shuhn)—resting

reluctantly (ri-LUHK-tuhnt-lee)—doing something you don't want to do unwillingly

DISCUSSION QUESTIONS

1. Was it fair for Evan's parents to ban skateboarding for the whole family after his brother was injured? Why or why not?

2. Should Evan have told his parents the truth about skateboarding sooner? What would you have done if you were in his position?

3. Why did Grandma give Evan the skateboard?

WRITING PROMPTS

1. Write about the relationship you have with a grandparent or another important older person in your life.

2. Pretend you are Chris, Evan's older brother. How do you think he feels about Evan skateboarding? Write a chapter from his point of view.

3. Evan decides to try the the eggplant during the competition, but he doesn't land it correctly. Write about a time you tried something but didn't succeed. How did you feel?

SKATEBOARDING

Make sure that whenever you're skateboarding, you're wearing the right safety equipment: a helmet and pads are a must!

THE OLLIE — The skateboarder pops the skateboard into the air so that it looks like the boarder is jumping with the skateboard attached to his or her feet.

KICKTURNS — A basic skateboarding skill that involves the skateboarder balancing on the back wheels of the board for a moment, and then swinging the front of the board in a new direction.

50-50 GRINDS — When a boarder grinds using both trucks. Trucks are the metal T-shaped parts mounted on the bottom of the skateboard deck and attached to the wheels. Normal skateboards have two trucks that face each other.

TRICKS

BOARD SLIDES — When a boarder skates alongside an object, usually a rail or curb, and ollies up onto it. The board lands sideways, balancing on the object, and the boarder slides along it.

ROCK N' ROLLS — When a skateboarder rides up a ramp, onto the lip, and then rides away. The front truck of the board goes over the lip of the ramp, and the bottom of the skateboard rests on the edge.

MANUALS — While rolling, a skateboarder lifts the front wheels of the board off the ground, making sure that the tail of the board doesn't touch the ground.

KICKFLIPS — A boarder flicks the board with the ball of his or her front foot, making it spin underfoot while in the air. The board spins over at least once in the air before the boarder lands comfortably, wheels down, and rides away.